To Denise,
with v. love, Jill xx.

Ozzee

the Dozy Mozzee

JILLIAN VIGRASS

Blue Poppy Publishing

7/7/2024

Layout by Oliver Tooley
Interior typeface – Century Schoolbook14pt
Cover typeface – Alvida, Trebuchet MS
Published by Blue Poppy Publishing
87 High Street, Ilfracombe, Devon, EX34 9NH

ISBN: 978-1-83778-032-7

A CIP catalogue record for this book is
available from the British Library

For my grandchildren Maisie, Arlo, and Rafe.

Contents

The Ozzee Rap, Part One

OZZEE the MOZZEE dozes all day,
When the sun goes down, she likes to play.
But she and her sisters, once it is night,
Must fly off to find some people to BITE.

1. First Bites

At the bottom of our village is a big pond. Around the rim grow leafy bushes, bulrushes and reeds. Cows and goats come there to drink. You may see jackals or warthogs, or even a snake on a low branch sucking up water. Herons, on their long legs, stroll about in the shallows.

The water is busy with buzzing insects. Dragonflies hover on their dazzling blue wings. Water boatmen skitter across the surface. Bees hum in the flowering bushes, collecting pollen, and then drop onto a bit of old log sticking out of the water for a drink.

One day, two mosquitoes, Ano and Feleez Mozzee, saw the pretty pond.

"What a good place to raise a family," said Feleez, waving her feelers. "No fish to gobble our eggs."

“Let’s make some babies right now,” replied Ano, rubbing his back legs together.

Soon the water was squiggling and squirming with tiny mosquito larvae.

Once all the larvae had changed into little mosquitoes, Ano and Feleez moved them to a new home, under the leaves of a bush that grew near the pond.

There were thirteen children, the little Mozzees. Eight were female children. Ano and Feleez named them: Buzzee, Cizzee, Dizzee, Fizzee, Lizzee, Maizee, and Tizzee. And last of all, there was Ozzee.

Five children were males. But Ano and Feleez were tired. They couldn’t think of any more names.

“I know,” said Ano, “let’s just call them all Mo. Mo 1, Mo 2, Mo 3, Mo 4 and Mo 5.” And so, the five males came to be known as the Five Mozzees named Mo.

In the mosquito world, it is the girls who have the hard, dangerous lives. Male mosquitoes live easily on the sap of bushes. But to be able to make baby mosquitoes, females must drink *human blood*.

One afternoon, the parents lined the girl Mozzees up on the branch of a bush by the pond.

"Today, children," said Feleez, "we're going to teach you how to find your own food. Buzzee, shush please! Now, what do girl mosquitoes like best?"

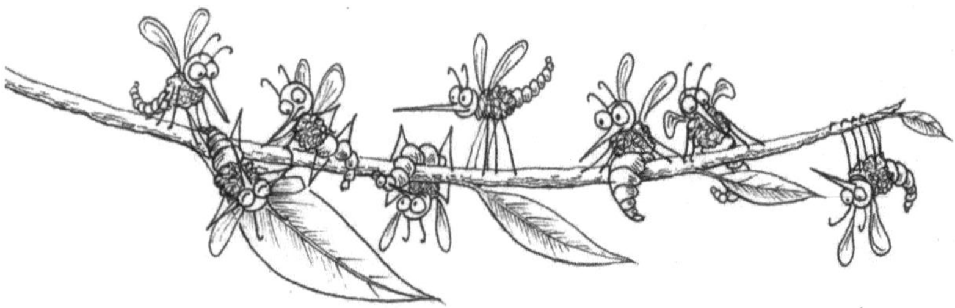

"Water?" asked Ozzee, who found the water in the pond tasty and sweet.

The other female Mozzees laughed so hard that Dizzee fell off the branch onto a leaf below.

"Dozy Ozzee!" buzzed Buzzee. But Ozzee didn't know what was funny.

"Please pay attention," said Ano. "Water is good to drink and we cannot live without it. But what is a female Mozzee's main food?"

"Blood!" Seven voices shouted at once. They flew off the stalk and whizzed around in the air crying, "Blood!"

But in Mozzee language it sounded like, "*Eeeeeyaouw!*"

Feleez called: "Come back. Settle down."

She waited till they were lined up on the stalk again. “And where is the best place to find it?” she asked.

“Elephants?” asked Ozzee.

“Elephants?” squeaked Cizzee. Once again, they all fell about laughing, so hard that Lizzee and Maizee fell off the branch and landed in the pond. It took them ages to get out, and then they had to sit apart, on another branch, and spread their stripy wings out to dry in the sun.

“They’ve got lots of blood, elephants have,” said Ozzee.

“Now, Ozzee, think a bit,” said Ano. “An elephant has very, very thick skin. How is a Mozzee going to pierce his skin with her little proboscis?”

“What’s a proboscis?” asked Ozzee.

“What’s a proboscis!” exclaimed Ano. “Can you believe this child? We talked about that yesterday. Where were you?”

“She was dozing,” said Maizee.

“Your proboscis is your long pointy mouth, through which you suck up water — and blood.”

Each of the other seven pointed her proboscis at Ozzee and buzzed. Ozzee didn't like this one bit. It felt scary.

"Stop, children," said Feleez. "Fizzee, where is the easiest place to find blood – the softest, thinnest skin to pierce with our thin, fragile proboscis?"

"Humans?" she answered.

"Humans," said Feleez. "So, this evening, at sunset, you girl Mozzees must get into pairs and set off to find humans. And when you find them, you must zoom in on them fast, pierce their skin with your proboscis and suck and drink as fast as you can."

"Fast!" echoed Ano. "Because if those humans feel you, they may try to stop you, and may even hit you."

"Yes," said Feleez, "swift as lightning must you strike."

As the sun started to go down, Feleez called them again.

"Now, find a partner."

All the little Mozzees quickly got into pairs. Fizzee had to be with Ozzee, and she was not pleased. The six others swooped and swizzled about in the air.

"*Zyooom!*" "*Eeeeaaayow!*"

"Off you go. Good luck!" Feleez called. Off they flew, all together. They looked like a little cloud.

But Ozzee was lounging on a lily pad in the pond, taking the odd sip of sweet water.

"Let's go," said Fizzee.

"In a minute," said Ozzee. "Don't rush me." Fizzee fizzed impatiently.

It was now twilight. Kenzi and his sister, Kimana, were playing in front of their house, pretending to be aeroplanes putting on an air show. They ran about with their arms out like wings.

"*Zyoooooom! Eeeeaaayow!*" they cried, running here and there. The six little Mozzees saw them and flew as fast as they could towards them.

"*Zyoooooom! Eeeeaaayow!*" screeched the little Mozzees, as they attacked. But they were moving too fast and it was difficult to land.

Hearing them, the children cried out: "AAGH!" and they waved their arms around their heads to shoo the Mozzees away. At that moment, the door opened and their mother, Maitu, called them.

"It's getting dark. Come inside. *Now*, before the mosquitoes attack you." The six Mozzees regrouped for a second attack, but the children had gone, and the door was firmly shut.

In front of the café, two men were having a drink at a table. They were engineers who had come to the village to build a bridge. The six Mozzees sat on the branch of a bush and looked at them. An electric light lit up the table and shone on the men's bare arms and ears. They were sitting still, talking. Perfect targets.

At a sign from Buzzee, the six attacked.

"Zyooom! Eeeeaaayow!"

The men jumped up. They brushed and swatted the mosquitoes away from their arms and heads and ran into the café.

The six regrouped on a branch.

"Anyone get any blood?" asked Tizzee. They shook their heads.

Meanwhile, Ozzee and Fizzee were just setting off. Ozzee hadn't practised zooming at all. She had been relaxing by the pond.

It was fully dark as they headed towards the village. No humans seemed to be outside. They passed the house of Kenzi and Kimana, shut tight, like the houses of their neighbours.

They came to the school. There they found a light on, and inside a classroom was a teacher, busy marking a pile of exercise books. His short sleeves left his arms perfectly exposed. Great! But as they tried to fly towards him, they banged into a solid, but invisible wall. Shaken and stunned, they tried to feel their way forward. Whatever it was that was stopping them, it was very smooth and very hard. They could see through it perfectly, but they couldn't go through it. What was it?

They started to inspect these large transparent walls from top to bottom and from side to side, but there was no way through.

"Let's go home now," said Ozzee.

"Let's try to find a way in," said Fizzee.

Just then, the teacher got up, and walked out of the door. Turning, he put a key in the lock, and pushed up the handle with his other hand.

"NOW!" screamed Fizzee, and she dived for his arm. It stretched forward like a landing strip, and Fizzee touched down half-way along. Without hesitating, she drove her proboscis into his soft skin, and sucked with all her might. The teacher's warm blood flowed into her hungry tummy, and a small gob of poison flowed into the teacher's arm.

"OW," exclaimed the teacher feeling a hot needle pierce his skin, but both his hands were busy. By the time he'd let go of the handle with his left hand and slapped his right arm, Fizzee had taken off again.

"*Ziiiyooooom!*" she crowed, "*Eeeaaayooow!*"

She flew round and round the teacher's head, as he swiped at her, and then flew back to Ozzee, laughing loudly. "You want to try, Ozzee?"

Ozzee looked at the angry teacher.

"No, no," she gulped, "he looks dangerous."

The teacher opened his bag and took out a jacket and a hat and put them on. He set off towards his home.

Ozzee was keen to go home, as she was hungry, and looking forward to sipping some sweet sap from the soft plants hanging over the pond. Fizzee fizzed around her in crazy circles, buzzing:

"*DOZY OZZEE! DOZY OZZEE!*"

The six others had no luck and soon they, too, headed home. But on the way, they came across the teacher walking along. They started to follow him, flying just above his head.

"Aha," said Buzzee, "here's a chance."

"Watch me!" cried Cizzee.

As light as air, she dropped onto the teacher's hat. The teacher walked on, humming a tune. Cizzee danced across the brim of the hat to the edge, swung around it, and disappeared underneath. The others held their breath. Cizzee crossed the underside of the brim to the teacher's face. Then she leant across, and without stepping onto his skin, she jabbed her proboscis into his temple, releasing her poison and sucking up his blood.

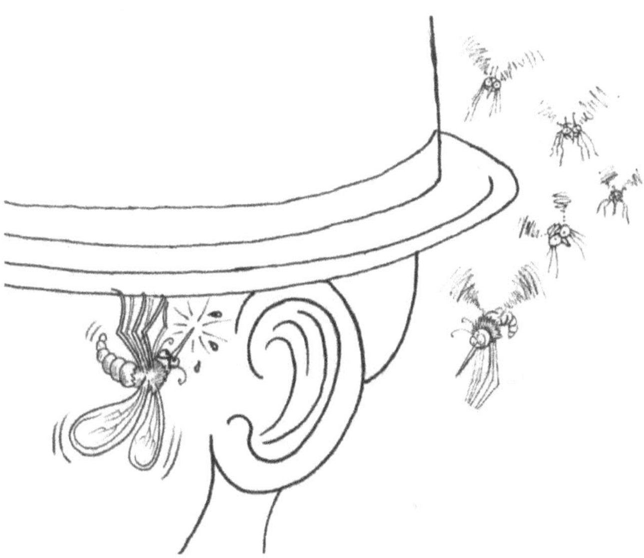

"Ow!" muttered the teacher, for the second time, and he smacked himself hard on the cheek.

"OOH!" the other Mozzees gasped.

But Cizzee was on the hat brim, and he missed her. Still, the force knocked her to the ground. The teacher hurried on. The five others flew down to help Cizzee. She was so shocked, they had to help her fly home to the pond. Hungry and cross, they moaned to their parents:

"Finding your own food is *hard*."

Only Fizzee was happy.

2. Buzzee Bites Mr Muscles

The following afternoon, as the sun dropped towards the land in the west and the sky went all pink, Ano and Feleez called the girl Mozzees for another lesson in finding blood to drink.

"First," said Feleez, "we told you to work in pairs. You did *not* listen. You worked as a swarm of six!"

"We worked as a pair," said Fizzee, "me and Ozzee."

"Yes, you did well," agreed Ano, "and you were able to suck the blood of the teacher."

"I did, too," said Cizzee.

"Yes," said Feleez, "but you nearly got smacked. How are you now?"

"Better, thanks," said Cizzee, stretching her stripy wings and admiring them.

"Not only did you work as a swarm, but you whizzed around, buzzing and whining, like the wind round a mountain. When you approached the playing children, what happened?"

"They heard us and ran indoors," said Maizee, looking a little bashful.

Ano smiled. "So, what will you do tonight?"

"Go in pairs."

"Make less noise."

By this time, the sun was sinking behind the mountain, and the sky was purple and red.

"Good – and use your brains," said Feleez. "Off you go."

The light was fading as Ozzee and Fizzee arrived at the home of Kimana and Kenzi. In the yard, Kenzi was kicking a ball about with his friend Billy. Kimana was sitting on a stool with her baby brother, watching them.

Ozzee was hungry. Baby looked chubby and sweet, his skin smooth and soft.

"I'll bite the baby," fizzed Fizzee. "You can bite the girl on her leg."

"That's not fair," whined Ozzee, as she flew down and hovered in the shadows below the hem of Kimana's skirt.

Silently, Fizzee landed on Baby's chubby cheek.

Slowly, Ozzee looked at Kimana's leg, trying to decide where to bite her.

"*Goo goo*," said Baby.

At that moment, Kimana felt Ozzee land on her ankle.

"*Oo*!" She looked down at her leg. Just as Ozzee got ready to attack, Kimana reached down and brushed her off.

And Fizzee sank her syringe-like proboscis into Baby's cheek and pulled and sucked, until the sweet taste filled her mouth. Baby tasted *so* much better than the teacher. Like a torch with a new battery, she felt her body light up.

Baby felt the sting, and he started to cry. Fizzee sank her needle into his cheek again. This was good!

"There, there," said Kimana, "what's the matter?"

Out came Maitu.

"Time to come in," she said. She took Baby asking: "Are you hungry?" She stepped into the light and saw the red blotches on Baby's cheek. "Ah, no. You've been bitten. Kimana, he's got a mosquito bite. Two bites! You should have come in earlier." Maitu soothed Baby. "Kenzi, come in now. Billy, you must go home."

Buzzee and Cizzee flew off to the village square. Outside the café were the two men, having a beer. But tonight, they were wearing trousers, long-sleeved shirts, shoes and socks. Only their hands and heads were exposed. Bother!

"I'll take the big, muscly man," buzzed Buzzee. The man's neck muscles bulged over his collar at the back.

"I'll take the long, bony man," hissed Cizzee. He was leaning backwards in his chair, one arm draped over the back of the chair next to his, his hand hanging down.

Silently, the two Mozzees moved into position and hovered quietly for a moment. Then Buzzee landed on Mr Muscles' collar and quickly sinking her proboscis into the skin of his neck, she spat in her saliva and sucked.

"Ouch! Mosquitoes," he said, slapping his neck, but Buzzee had already buzzed off.

Softer than a breath, Cizzee dropped onto Mr Lanky's hand. Her feet were so light that he didn't feel them. She paused and then plunged her needle at his knuckle. But it was hard. The skin was tough, and the bone was just under the surface.

She tried again, but the man felt it, and snatching his hand from the back of the chair, brushed it with his other hand, sweeping Cizzee off. She landed, *again,* in the dust on the ground.

Dizzee and Lizzee came across Billy, walking home with his ball under his arm. He was only wearing shorts and a tee-shirt. They decided to take an arm each. Dizzee whizzed in and sank her needle into the arm that was carrying the ball, just as Lizzee did the same to the arm that was not.

"OW!" yelled Billy, as the hot sting hit both arms at the same time, and he dropped the ball. His mother came out of the house and saw him.

"Ow!" said Billy again, "I've been bitten."

"Billy," said Mama, "you must be home before dusk, when the mosquitoes come out. How many times must I tell you?"

"It's OK, Mama," he said, "it doesn't really hurt."

Maizee and Tizzee went to the school. They, too, were attracted by the light of the windows, but found themselves stopped by the glass wall. Inside, the teacher was busy marking his books. They could not find a way in. They waited, but when the teacher left, he put on a jacket, as well as his hat.

"I'll have to bite his face, like Cizzee," whispered Maizee.

"No, bite his hand," replied Tizzee.

The teacher moved into position to lock the classroom door. Maizee hovered above his arm and then – ! – she attacked.

"Ugh!"

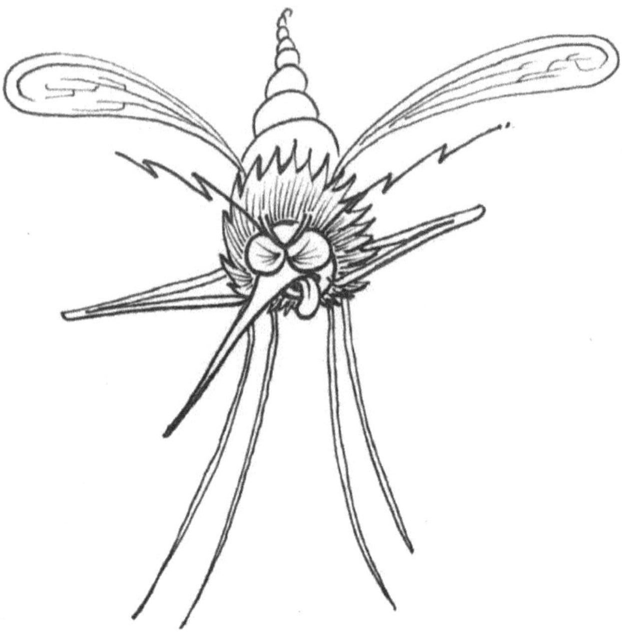

The man had put a bitter cream on his skin that tasted like poison. She sprang off the teacher's hand in disgust. The teacher locked the door and set off for home.

When the Mozzees got home that night, four had managed to feed, but not Cizzee, Tizzee or Maizee, nor, of course, Ozzee, and they were very hungry.

But Ano and Feleez said their children were making progress.

3. Nip, Bite! Nip, Hide!

The next afternoon, they gathered the family a little earlier. The sun was still above the trees.

"Now, children," said Ano, "yesterday you had some success. But Maizee had a bad experience. The teacher had put cream on his skin to protect himself. From you. This cream has a bitter taste and is poisonous for us to eat."

"When you start to succeed in biting humans," said Feleez, "two things will happen. They will go inside earlier, as soon as it starts to get dark, and those who don't will cover themselves in clothing, or in this cream."

"We will be hungry," moaned Ozzee.

"No, Ozzee," said Feleez, with a smile, "you have to wake up a bit, start out earlier."

"And," said Ano, "you have to start making plans. Be clever and daring."

"Uh-oh!" said Tizzee.

"So today," said Feleez, "you must set off when the sun starts sinking. You must go to the houses or the school *before* it gets dark."

"But how can we bite the humans before dark?" cried Maizee.

Maizee was quite right. Anopheles mosquitoes do not bite humans until it gets dark.

"You nip inside the house before they close up, and find a hiding place, in a corner or under a table, and then you wait until it gets dark."

"Nip inside, hide. Nip a human, hide." said Ano.

Nip inside, hide! – Nip a human, hide!

"Nip, hide! Nip, hide!" The Mozzees all sang together and jumped up and down on the branch.

"Why do we have to hide after biting them?" asked Cizzee.

"Good question. Because once we have bitten humans, they hunt for us and try to hit us and squash us. The most dangerous time is after biting. You must retreat quickly to a good hiding place."

"Yes, remember the sad story of your cousin Stinger, who bit a woman and then went and sat in the middle of a white wall. The woman whacked him with her shoe, and that was the end of Stinger. Don't sit in the middle of a wall, especially after biting. Hide yourself."

"After biting and drinking and hiding, what do we do?" asked Fizzee. "How do we leave the house to come home?"

"Well," said Ano, "you may have to wait until the morning, when the humans open up their houses."

The little Mozzees did *not* like that. They all started whining.

"But," said Feleez, "there is one way it can help you. If you are patient, the humans will go to bed and sleep. And then, you can drink from them more safely."

Ozzee thought it sounded scary and wished she could be a male Mozzee, who could doze in the sun all day, sip some sweet sap from the plants, and then play happily all night long.

Off flew the Mozzees, hither and thither, already hungry and eager to eat. As usual, Ozzee was last to get ready, and Fizzee was very hungry.

"Come *on,* Ozzee," she fizzed. But Ozzee was not in a rush, because she had a plan. Find a safe place and doze until all the humans slept. Then bite them while they were asleep. *Eazzzy* …

They flew straight to the house of Kimana and Kenzi, who were still playing outside. They didn't stop, but flew through the open door, into the house.

What a different world it was inside! Instead of the curving, irregular shapes of nature, everything was oblong – oblong bed, oblong table, oblong pictures on the wall. And the strange new smells of human food (like chicken stew, pineapple, and chocolate cake.)

Fizzee's plan was to suck blood as soon as possible, and she went and sat on top of a picture frame, where she had a good view. She would wait until the family were all inside and find the first good moment to strike.

As Ozzee planned, she found a soft white curtain, a perfect place for a snooze. She crept into one of its folds, and soon dozed off.

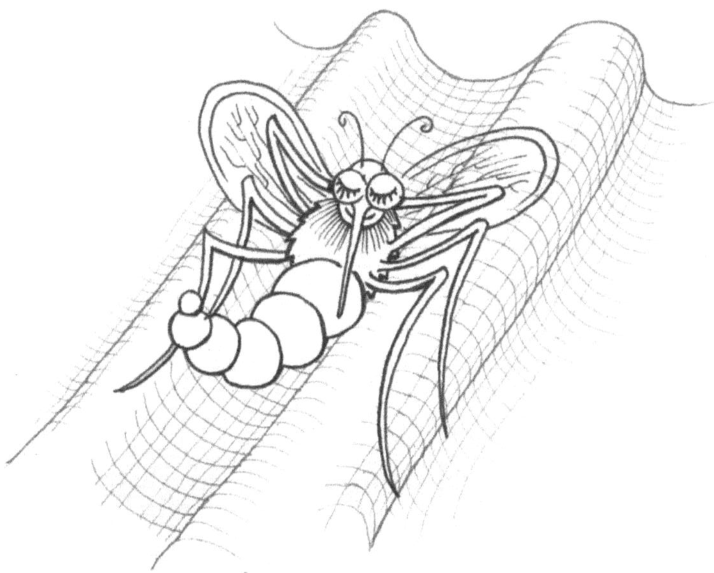

Meanwhile, the other Mozzees were moving across the village. Cizzee and Buzzee came to Billy's house. The door was shut, but Billy was still outside, playing with his dog, Bouncer, so they waited.

Soon, Billy's mother opened the door.

"Time to come in," she called. Billy was throwing a stick for Bouncer, who dashed after it joyfully, and galloped back in no time, dropping it at Billy's feet and yapping at him to throw it again.

"*Now*, Billy," called Mama, and went inside, leaving the door open. Cizzee and Buzzee nipped inside. They, too, were amazed by the strange objects and smells found in human houses. One of the oblongs showed a moving picture of elephants eating and drinking; it gave off a lot of light. Cizzee and Buzzee were drawn to this pretty light, but when they got close it was too strong. So, they settled on the wall behind it, hidden by its shadow.

Mama was busy at the hot oblong thing, where food was bubbling in a pot.

After a while, she went back to the door and this time she yelled, "BILLY, come in right NOW!"

Sadly, Billy left Bouncer and his stick, and came inside. He flopped down on the soft oblong (which was a sofa) and began to watch the moving pictures. Buzzee flew above him. Billy relaxed, his head propped on his hand, absorbed by the elephants. His bare legs stretched out invitingly. Buzzee remembered her parents' words:

"Plan. Be clever. Nip. Hide."

She dropped down onto the sofa next to Billy's right leg and examined it. At the bottom of the leg, where it came to the foot, there were nice big veins near the surface. She could feel the warmth of this river under Billy's skin. Carefully she flew up into the air above the ankle, and then, dropping down quickly, she drilled through the skin, into the vein. On the moving picture, two elephants were fighting. Billy didn't notice Buzzee, taking a slow drink from his ankle.

Cizzee nipped under the table and hid there. It was dark and she felt safe. After some time, Billy and Mama sat down to eat. Cizzee bit Mama on her leg and on her foot. Like Billy, Mama didn't seem to feel it, but a few minutes later, she reached down to rub and scratch her foot.

"I think I've been bitten," she said.

"Me too," said Billy, whose ankle now had a big, itchy bump on it.

"I can't see any mosquitoes," said Mama, looking around the room, ready to whack any she could find. But Cizzee was tucked into the corner underneath the table, and Buzzee was snoozing behind the moving picture oblong, which was now showing a car chase.

Maizee and Tizzee decided to try their luck at the school again. When they got there, the teacher was inside, talking with another teacher, and the door was shut. But when they flew closer to look through the invisible wall, they found there was an opening in it, and in no time they were inside.

Pleased with themselves, they flew around and around the room. Soon, the movement caught the teacher's eye.

"I'd better shut the window," he said, and he got up and closed it tightly.

The two Mozzees dropped behind one of the children's desks and kept quiet in a shadow. The teacher sat down and continued talking. Maizee flew under the desks until she got to the front one.

The second teacher was wearing a skirt and her legs were bare. Maizee flew to the dark space under her chair. Without hesitating, she aimed for the back of the woman's calf muscle, and plunged her proboscis in, drinking as fast as she could. She was very hungry, and the woman's leg had a sweet smell of the lotion she used after her bath. Her skin was smooth and hairless, and Maizee remembered the hairy hand she had tried to drink from the night before at the café. This was so much nicer.

The woman teacher reacted to the poison, uncrossed her legs, and reached down to scratch her calf muscle. Maizee jumped away and flew back to hide under the desks.

The woman got up. "Too many mosquitoes about," she said and she left.

The teacher opened a book and started marking it. Tizzee moved to the front and looked down on him from the top of the big board on the wall. With his head bent forward, the teacher was showing an open stretch of neck. She hoped it didn't have any horrid cream on it.

Tizzee launched herself, wings folded back. Her needle easily pierced the teacher's skin, and she started to drink. But he felt her and slapped his neck. Terrified, she jumped away and then flew furiously round his head, whining like a drill. The teacher slapped at the air and missed.

Tizzee came in again, like a fighter jet. "*Niiiuuooow!*"

The teacher jumped up, swiping at her wildly with a book.

And then Tizzee made a terrible mistake. She saw the wall and landed on it.

SWAT.

Maizee closed her eyes in horror. But when she opened them, Tizzee was *not* stuck to the wall, flat and broken, like Stinger. She had just vanished. Where *was* she?

In the meantime, Lizzee and Dizzee headed for the square. It was still light when they got there, so they did as they were told, and flew into the café. But when the workers arrived, they sat outside as usual. So, the Mozzees went out again and landed in the tree overhanging the table.

The men ordered drinks and sat about talking. It got dark, and the Mozzees started to plan their attack.

Mr Lanky was wearing a long-sleeved shirt, but like the day before, he liked to lean back in his chair and stretch his arm along the chair next to him.

Lizzee looked at the back of his hand. It didn't look very tasty. But then she noticed skin between the man's fingers. Silently she hovered over the hand. The side skin of the fingers looked softer. She alighted lightly on his finger.

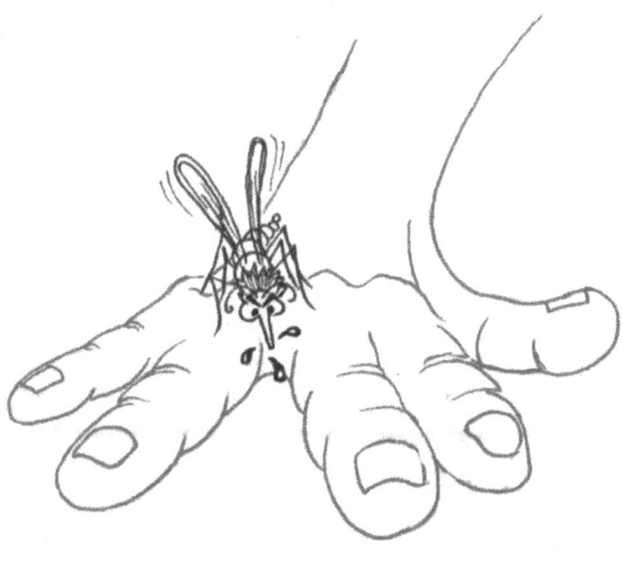

Yes, she was able to pierce it softly, so that the man didn't feel it. She took three small sips and one long suck, from different places, and then quietly flew off, back into the tree.

Mr Muscles was wearing a thick jacket.

"You feeling cold, Muscles?" asked Mr Lanky.

"Brrr. Yes. It's cool tonight. Aren't you cold?"

"No, it seems the same as last night to me."

The jacket had a high collar, and Dizzee couldn't see how she was going to bite him at all. She waited. The men talked and sipped their drinks. After a while, the big man unzipped his jacket. Then Mr Lanky said he was going to get another drink. What would his friend like?

"Something cold, with ice," replied Mr Muscles.

"I thought you were feeling cold?"

"I was. But now I feel hot. The first drink warmed me up."

He took his jacket off and hung it on the back of the chair. Now he was just in a t-shirt. In the tree above, Dizzee pointed her proboscis at him.

Mr Lanky came back with two drinks, and Mr Muscles put his elbows on the table and leaned forward, talking to his friend as he drank and sucked on the ice. Dizzee dropped from the tree and hovered behind him, then zoomed in on his big, bare upper arm. Lizzee joined in, on the other arm. Soon they were both sucking his blood happily, while he swigged his drink. After a while, he scratched his upper arms and then shuddered.

"You know, I don't feel too good," he said. "I think I'll go and sleep now."

He got up, took his jacket, and left. Back in the tree, Dizzee and Lizzee looked at each other.

"That was odd," said Dizzee.

"Yes," said Lizzee, "his skin was *damp*."

4. Ozzee Trapped

Very early the next morning, Ozzee woke up in the fold of the soft white curtain. She was very hungry and now was the time to put her plan into action. The human family were all asleep and she could hear the soft rise and fall of their breathing. She stretched and then flew up to the lamp shade. Looking down, she could see Maitu and Baby, sleeping soundly, and she rubbed her front feet together happily.

But then she noticed something. The nice soft white curtain, where she had slept, had moved. It was now stretched around the bed, and the woman and baby were inside it.

There must be a way through it. She flew all around the bed, but could find no way in.

Oh bother! What could she do? She'd have to go for the children. She flew to the room next door.

Sure enough, there were the two children, sleeping peacefully. Kenzi was half out of his covers and looked an easy target.

But no. They too were safely inside a net curtain.

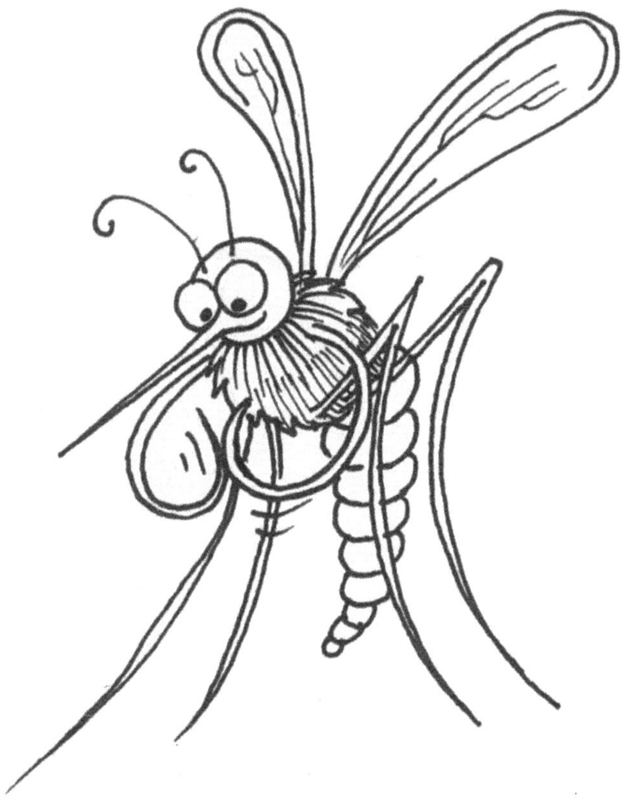

Round and round the beds flew Ozzee, looking for a way in. She was getting more and more hungry. She dive-bombed the white netting, making her loudest dive bomber noises.

"*VREEEOOOYOOOM.*"

She hit the soft wall and bounced. Making her highest whines, she tore around the room.

"*IYIYIYIYIYIYIY.*"

Kimana stirred in her sleep. She flung out an arm and mumbled.

Ozzee was SO hungry. Ozzee was SO angry.

Again, she dive-bombed the curtain, dropping at her highest speed from near the ceiling, her proboscis pointing ahead like a drill. And this time, it went through one of the holes in the net.

YES!

But *No-o-o.* Her face bounced against the mesh, and there she stopped, her proboscis sticking through the net, the rest of her still on the outside. She pushed with her feet, to reverse. She couldn't pull back. Her head was stuck. NO! The net had nabbed her.

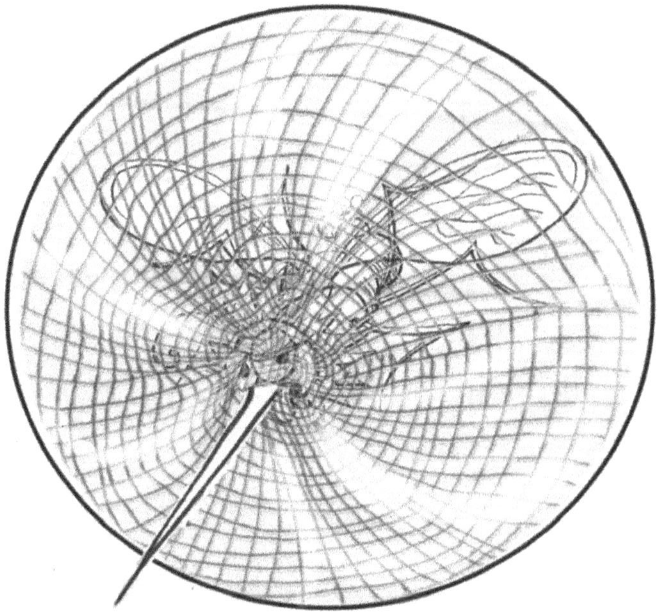

Billy and Mama had no net curtains to sleep under. So, in the middle of the night, Buzzee and Cizzee were able to drink from them while they slept. This time, Cizzee bit Billy, and Buzzee bit Mama. The two humans stirred and mumbled, but they didn't wake up.

In the morning, Mama got up as soon as it got light. She had itchy bumps on her arms and face. She opened the door and windows to let in the air.

Quickly the two Mozzees nipped out and flew home to their pond, feeling nice and full.

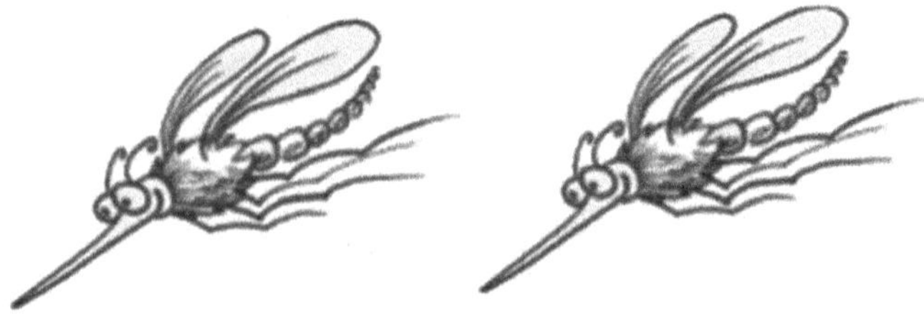

When Fizzee woke up, after a long sleep, and stretched her wings, she could see the first rays of light sneaking in round the curtains. Time to go.

Where was Ozzee? She flew round the big room, but no, Ozzee wasn't there. She went to the bedroom where the mother and baby were sleeping, but there was no sign of Ozzee there. Then she went to the children's bedroom and there was poor Ozzee, caught by her proboscis in the netting.

"Oh Ozzee," she sighed, "you dozy mozzee."

Ozzee whined loudly. She batted her wings as fast as she could, trying to reverse, but no such luck. She was stuck. Fizzee flew behind her and held her tail with her front feet and tried to fly, pulling Ozzee. No, she wasn't strong enough. Ozzee was really stuck.

Fizzee fizzed with frustration. She flew madly around the room, trying to think what to do.

When the children woke up, there was a big chance they would find Ozzee, and then, what would they do to her?

Just then, Baby woke up and started to chatter. Fizzee heard the woman talking to the baby and then footsteps. In she came to wake her children up. Oh no! Fizzee dropped under the bed and hid. Maitu didn't see Ozzee. Phew! But the danger was still huge. Kenzi and Kimana would get up any minute and one of them might spot Ozzee sitting on the net. Did *anyone* have a sister as annoying as Ozzee?

She had to get help.

"Ozzee, I'm going home as soon as the door opens," she said.

"No," wailed Ozzee, "please don't leave me."

"I'll go back and fetch the others to help free you. Just wait quietly."

Away she went, leaving poor Ozzee stuck in the mosquito net.

When Fizzee arrived back at the pond, she found the other Mozzees gathered around their parents. They were buzzing loudly.

"I bit three humans."

"I bit a man."

"I bit a girl."

"I bit a baby and he tasted amazing."

Just then, Maizee and Tizzee arrived, with the news that Tizzee had bitten the teacher, who had almost swatted her. The others listened, scared and shocked.

Fizzee sat on a stalk, waiting impatiently to tell them about Ozzee, and that they must come and help with the rescue. But as the sun warmed her wings, she started to yawn. She felt drowsy and soon she drifted away into sleep.

5. Fizzee to the Rescue

The day was hot. The Mozzees felt hot. The dogs, feeling hot, crawled under bushes and lay there, panting. The cows found shade under trees. At school, the children in the classrooms felt weak and couldn't listen to their teachers. The workmen who had come to build the new bridge, sweated in the sun.

But not everyone felt hot. Mr Muscles was not at work at the bridge. He was in his room feeling very cold, with a blue blanket wrapped around him. Inside his body, inside his blood vessels, were thousands of tiny parasites.

They loved living inside Mr Muscles' big, spacious body, and they were having millions of little baby parasites. They enjoyed travelling all over the place inside him, carried along in his arteries and veins, and they were all feeding on his blood cells.

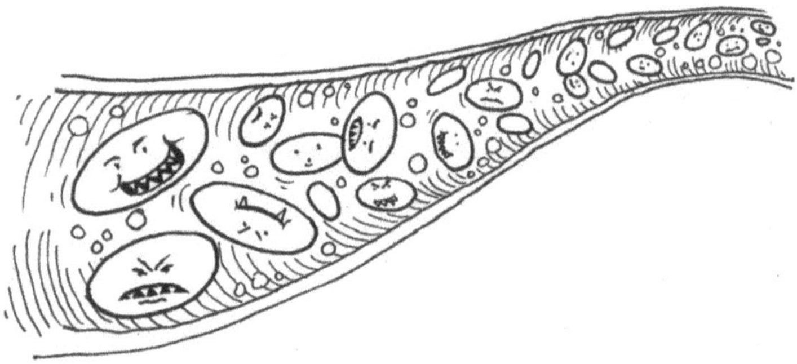

Now, Mr Muscles' body didn't like having all these visitors, so it decided to heat itself up, to kill them. His brain told all the cells in his body: *You feel cold! You feel very co-o-old. Warm up! Warm up!* He started to shiver and pulled the blue blanket around him. His teeth chattered. His skin was covered in goose flesh.

He shivered and shuddered, and his head ached. He sat on his bed, shivering on the hottest day for months. He felt so sick.

He had an illness called malaria. He had caught it when a mosquito bit him in his home town, far away.

The more his muscles shivered, however, the more heat they made. Mr Muscles began to feel less cold. He started to feel nice and warm. He lay on the bed and drifted off to sleep. Some time later, he woke up. He was hot, so very hot. He threw off the blanket and took off his clothes. His head was hurting badly. He was burning with fever.

Fizzee woke up at midday, when the sun got too hot, and dropped down to the pond for a drink. The water was sweet and cool. She looked at her reflection, her long proboscis and her big eyes. Her face in the water looked like Ozzee's face.

"Ozzee!"

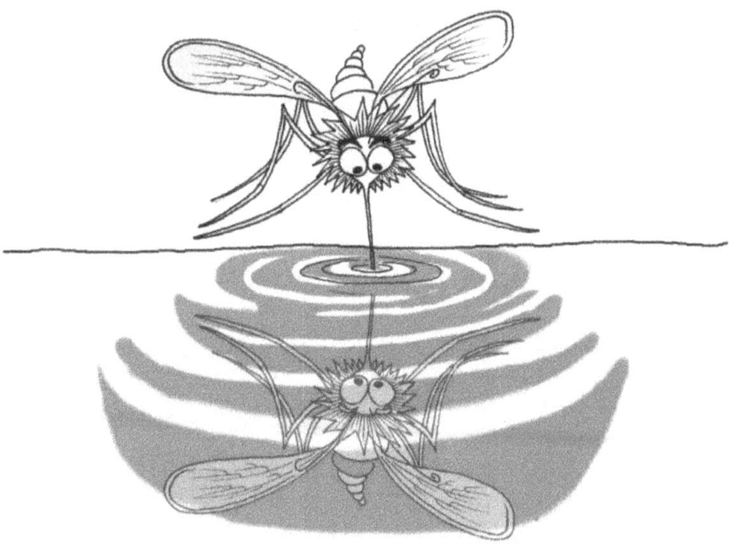

She flew up to the bush where the other Mozzees were dozing in the shade.

"Wake up. Wake up!" she screeched.

"What is it?" they buzzed back lazily.

"Ozzee. It's Ozzee. She's stuck. Caught. Trapped. In a house. In a NET thing."

Much grumbly buzzing followed this announcement.

"Wake up," Fizzee pleaded. "We must rescue Ozzee."

More grumbly buzzing followed. Fizzee's sisters were still sleepy.

Fizzee flew up above the bush. She hovered there for a moment, and then, folding back her wings, dropped at high speed over the twig where her sisters slept, whining as loudly as she could.

"Buzz off, Fizzee," said Buzzee. "Go and rest."

Fizzee *fumed.* But someone had heard her.

The five Mozzees named Mo were never tired. The boy Mozzees didn't have to fly all night over the village, finding humans to bite. They fed on the sap of their bushes and reeds whenever they were hungry.

"Something's up," buzzed Mo 1.

"Why's Fizzee fussing when she should be resting?" whined Mo 2.

"Why don't you ask her?" asked Mo 3.

"Why don't you?" whined Mo 2.

"Well, someone do it," muttered Mo 4.

"I'll go," sighed Mo 5. He flew up off his branch. "Fizzee, Fizzee, what's the matter?" he called.

"Oh, Mo 5, Ozzee is trapped in a house. We must rescue her, but my sisters are all tired. Look at them snoring there under that big leaf."

"Caught? How?" asked Mo 5.

"She's caught in a big white soft thing with holes."

"Oh?" Mo 5 laughed. "How did that happen?"

"It's not funny." The many lenses of her large eyes sprinkled tears. "She's caught tight around her face, her proboscis on the inside. She's stuck ... can't get free."

"Don't cry, Fizzee. I'll speak to my brothers." Mo 5 flew back to his branch while Fizzee fretted on a reed.

"Hey guys?" he called. "We are needed. Ozzee, that dozy Mozzee, has got caught in a human house, and we have to help Fizzee to rescue her."

Mo 1 looked up. Life was dull for young male Mozzees. He dreamed of action.

"Is that a task for Five Mozzees named Mo?" he called to his brothers.

Mozzees 2, 3 and 4 started to hum.

"Who can bring poor Ozzee home?" sang Mo1.

His brothers sat up.

"Five Mozzees named Mo!"

"Fizzee, you are not alone."

"Five Mozzees named Mo!"

"Who can bring poor Ozzee home?"
"Five Mozzees named Mo!"

Five minutes later, off they flew. Fizzee flew in front, with the Five Mos behind her in a V-shape, like ducks.

They sang as they went.

"Five Mos fly," sang Mo 1.

"Five Mos fly," echoed his four brothers.

"High in the sky."

"High in the sky."

But Fizzee did not join in. She was too anxious about Ozzee.

In a short time, they arrived at Kimana and Kenzi's house. They were at school. Maitu was sitting out under the big tree with Baby. The Mozzees landed on a bush.

The door was open.

"It's in there," said Fizzee.

"It looks dark," whined Mo 2.

"Scary," said Mo 3.

Fizzee fizzed and fumed at her brothers.

"Are you going to help me, or not?" she demanded.

"I'm with you, Sister," said Mo 1.

"So am I," said Mo 5, "lead on, Fizz."

"Follow me," said Fizzee, heading towards the open door, with Mo 1 and Mo 5 behind her. She flew to the bedroom. Inside, the room had changed. The beds were neatly made. The nets were tied back.

"Ozzee? Ozzee?" called Fizzee, "where are you?" There was no reply. "Ozzee, where are you?"

Then she heard a soft "*zzzz*."

There in the corner, dangling from the net by her proboscis, was Ozzee – sound asleep! Fizzee landed beside Ozzee on the net.

"Ozzee? Ozzee? Wake up." Ozzee opened one eye.

"Ozzee, we're here to rescue you. Wake up."

"Too hungry," murmured Ozzee, and closed her eye again.

"Wake UP." Fizzee bounced up and down on the net. "WAKE UP!"

"I'm dozing," said Ozzee. Poor Ozzee, the net had poison on it, like the cream the teacher used, and it was making her feel ill.

Fizzee looked at Mo 1.

"What can we do?"

"Carry her? Pull her out, then carry her?"

"I'll fetch the others," said Mo 5, helpfully. Off he flew.

Ten minutes later, the six Mozzees sat on the net next to Ozzee and made a plan.

"We each take one of her six legs and we pull," said Mo 1. So, with their front feet, they each took one of Ozzee's legs.

"Now!" said Mo 1. With a loud whirring of their wings, the Mozzees tried to fly away from the net, pulling Ozzee.

“Ow! OW! **OW!**” Poor Ozzee. Her proboscis was stuck fast.

“Stop,” said Fizzee. “We’re hurting her. This doesn’t work.”

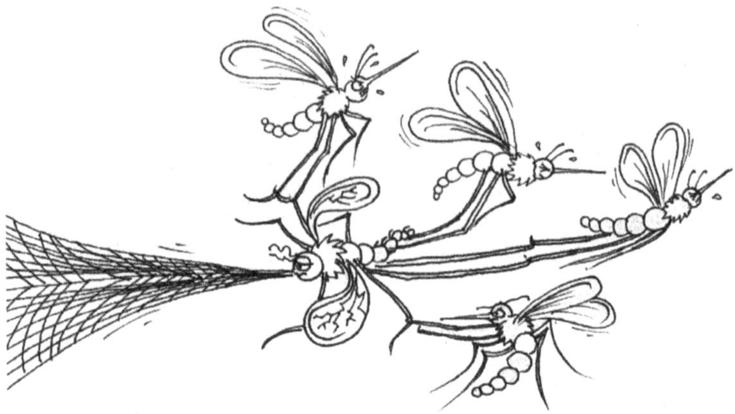

Then Mo 3 had an idea.

“We need to open the hole. Mo 2 and Mo 4, you get on either side of Ozzee and pull the net away from her proboscis.”

With their front feet, Mo 2 and Mo 4 grasped the net on either side of Mozzee’s face and pulled in opposite directions. Once again, with a *louder* whirring of wings, the other Mozzees tried to fly away from the net, tugging Ozzee with all their might. Her proboscis was still stuck fast.

At that moment, Maitu came into the room to put clean clothes in the drawer, and she heard the buzzing of the Mozzees.

"Oh, no. Mosquitoes," she exclaimed, and hurried off to fetch the insect spray.

"DANGER!" said Fizzee. "We *must* hurry."

"Fizzee," said Mo 5. "Spit on the net. Wet it so her proboscis can slip out when we pull."

At once, Fizzee landed next to Ozzee's face and started spitting. Mo 2 and Mo 4 pulled and pulled at the net. Fizzee kept spitting and spitting. Mo 1 and Mo 3 tugged and tugged at Ozzee's back legs. Mo 5 yanked her tail.

Fizzee saw Ozzee's proboscis slip a bit, and then another bit. And then, suddenly, it shot out. Ozzee was *FREE*.

"Come, Ozzee, fly now," fizzed Fizzee.

"I'm tired," said Ozzee, too weak to try.

"Oh, *please,"* begged Fizzee. *"Please try."*

"I can't."

There was only one thing for it. They would have to carry her. So, Mo 2, Mo 3, Mo 4 and Mo 5 got under Ozzee's body. Mo 1 and Fizzee each took one of Ozzee's limp wings, stretched it out and held it open. With great effort they pulled the load off the net. Slowly, with a lot of buzzing, they flew up and towards the bedroom door. At that moment, Maitu came back in – brandishing her insect spray. As she raised her arm to swat, the Mozzees buzzed over her shoulder. They flew through the kitchen and out into the sunlight.

Carrying Ozzee was hard work. She was floppy and helpless. Fizzee looked at the Five Mos, struggling to fly with their heavy burden. They were flapping their wings so fast that all you could see was a blur. But they were going very slowly, and a soft breeze was pushing them sideways.

"Go to the left," she panted. "We're being blown off course!"

Her brothers buzzed and whined in annoyance. Ozzee was feeling heavier, and **heavier** and **HEAVIER** by the minute.

"Five Mos fly ... " puffed Fizzee, encouragingly. There was no reply. "Come on guys ... try ... sing ... FIVE MOS FLY."

"Five ... fly," came the feeble response.

"HIGH in the SKY."

"High ..." gasped Mo 1 and Mo 2.

But looking ahead, they could see the ground coming closer and closer.

"Going *down* ... *need* ... STOP," groaned Mo 5.

"*Aaagh* ..."

They bumped down near a bush in a vegetable plot, landing Ozzee on a small potato leaf lying on the ground. They looked at each, and then at her, and sighed.

"Ozzee," gasped Mo 1, "you *have* to make *some* effort. You've got to fly *a bit.* We'll help you, but you *have* to help us."

"I *can't.*"

"You've *got* to."

"*Can't,*" she wailed.

"You *MUST.* Otherwise we'll never get home. *Please try,*" they buzzed at her angrily.

Ozzee turned her head away. Her proboscis flopped limply.

Fizzee flew onto a branch. What was the use of chivvying her? Ozzee may be lazy and obstinate. Or she may be truly starving and ill. Who knew? She looked down at her brothers, still prodding Ozzee and pleading with her. What a waste of time! Ozzee looked quite comfortable, lying on her leaf, ignoring them all.

And then Fizzee had an idea. An idea that she thought just might work ...

"Hey, guys," she called, dropping down beside them, "why don't we try this?" And she started to explain.

Some time later, Cizzee woke up from a deep sleep to see a strange sight. Flying towards her was an enormous insect.

"HELP!" she screamed.

Buzzee and her sisters woke up. So did Ano and Feleez. They looked at this monster insect. It had many heads, many eyes, and many wings. It was flying very slowly but buzzing as loudly as a bee. It was flying straight at them.

"HIDE!" yelled Lizzee.

"Wait," said Feleez. It was a strange sight, but it seemed that her children were all flying in a joined-up clump. And yes, there were the Five Mos. And there was Fizzee. They were carrying a leaf. And flopped on the leaf was Ozzee.

At that moment, a breath of evening breeze blew on the group, almost halting it. It looked as if the leaf bearers would tumble to the ground. The sisters gasped.

"HELP THEM," ordered Ano. "GO!"

Off whizzed the seven sisters. They zoomed in on the flailing group, each getting a shoulder under the leaf that bore poor Ozzee, who – it must be said – looked rather comfortable lying there, reclining like a royal princess.

The rescue party landed with a bump on the branch. The Mozzee family buzzed around them. When they heard Fizzee's story, they all made a big whirring noise with their wings, which is the Mozzee way of clapping.

Ozzee was floppy with hunger and thirst. Her sisters brought her sap from the leaves. When she felt better, she told her story. She got a big lecture from Ano and Feleez. But she didn't mind. She was so happy to be safely home by the pond.

"I'll never try to bite humans again," said Ozzee. "I'm staying with the boys."

And she dozed off.

6. The Six Ozzee Rules

"What a good story," exclaimed Mrs Moyo, the teacher. "I like a happy ending. It must have taken you hours to write it, Kenzi."

Kenzi closed his book and smiled happily, but suddenly Kimana stuck her hand up really urgently.

"But Miss," she exclaimed, "It's not a happy ending. Not for the humans in the story."

"Oh? Well, why don't you explain?"

Kimana stood thinking for a while before she spoke:

"In the story, when Buzzee bit Mr Muscles, the big man was ill with malaria. He had lots of little creatures, called parasites, living in his bloodstream. So

Buzzee must have drunk these creatures along with his blood.

"The next day, Buzzee went to Billy's house, where she bit Billy, first, and then Billy's mother. Buzzee must have passed the parasites to them, because one morning, two weeks ago, when his mother went to wake Billy up for school, he said he felt cold and had a headache. But when she felt his forehead he was burning hot with fever. So, he stayed in bed, wrapped in his red blanket, with his teeth chattering.

"Later she started to feel cold, too. Soon her head was aching and her teeth were chattering. They both have malaria."

"It's true," said Kenzi, "Buzzee bit other people, giving them malaria. Dizzee and Lizzee also bit Mr Muscles, and so they, too, spread the illness. Teachers and parents and children have got sick. And the baby next door is very ill in hospital with it ..."

Kenzi paused. A tear ran down his cheek.

"And Billy is really ill. He's too ill to play ball and too ill to come to school – and – so I wrote him this story. But I don't know the ending ..."

Mrs Moyo spoke in a kind voice. "Yes, Kenzi. It's a bad illness. For babies and little children malaria is very dangerous. But for your age group, too, for you primary school children, it is still dangerous. It can damage your eyes, your ears, and even your brain. But let's try and finish your story together."

On the blackboard, Mrs Moyo drew a huge Ozzee, with a long proboscis, huge round eyes, wide, lacy wings, and six long legs.

"Now," she asked, "in the story, there were actions that people took to avoid getting bitten. What were they?"

Juma put his hand up.

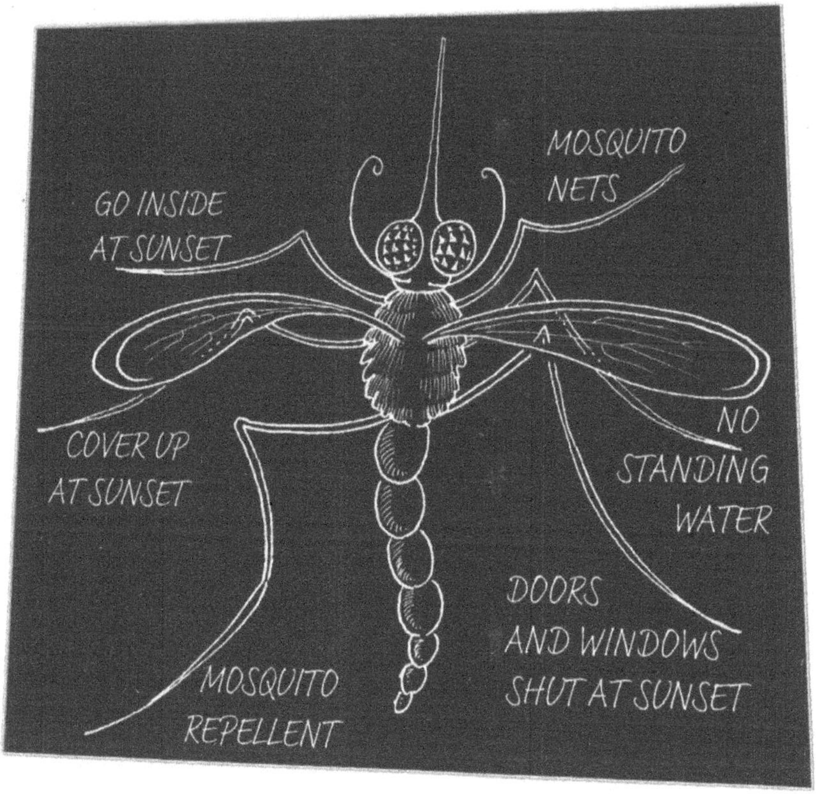
GO INSIDE
AT SUNSET
MOSQUITO
NETS
COVER UP
AT SUNSET
NO
STANDING
WATER
DOORS
AND WINDOWS
SHUT AT SUNSET
MOSQUITO
REPELLENT

"They went inside when it started to get dark."

"GO INSIDE AT SUNSET," Mrs Moyo wrote next to Ozzee's left front foot. "Lena?"

"Wear long sleeves and trousers, if you are outside after dark," Lena said.

"COVER UP AT SUNSET," wrote Mrs Moyo, next to Ozzee's left middle foot. "Moses?"

"Put on cream to stop them biting you," said Moses.

"MOSQUITO REPELLENT," wrote Mrs Moyo next to Ozzee's left back foot.

"Shut the windows and doors after dark," offered Abigail.

"DOORS AND WINDOWS SHUT AT SUNSET," wrote Mrs Moyo, next to Ozzee's right back foot.

"What else can you do?" Mrs Moyo asked.

The class looked back at her, trying to think.

"Where do mosquitoes lay their larvae?" she asked them.

"In water," replied Kenzi.

"Well then? You should **not** have puddles and pools of water around your house. Even an old pan with rainwater can house hundreds of mosquito larvae."

"NO STANDING WATER," she wrote next to Ozzee's middle right foot.

"And the most helpful thing of all?" She looked at the class. They looked back at her. "Mosquitoes find it easiest to bite us when we're asleep. What did Kimana and Kenzi have that stopped them getting bitten in their sleep?" she asked.

"Nets," replied Kimana, "we have mosquito nets."

"MOSQUITO NETS," wrote Mrs Moyo, next to Ozzee's front right foot. "*All* you children *must* sleep under nets, especially in the rainy season."

She started a new drawing, of a little child in a cot with a mosquito net over it. Around the net, she sketched lots of mosquitoes unable to get in, while the child slept peacefully and safely inside.

The children looked at the giant Ozzee and the cot beset by Mozzees.

"When I was little," said Mrs Moyo, "my father got very sick with malaria, so he went to the clinic. The doctor told him that mosquitoes give it to us when they bite us in our sleep. We should all sleep under nets. So he went to the shop, but all he could afford was one net.

"He hung it above my grandfather's bed; as the elder of the family he had the right to it. But Grandpa made him take it down. '*Put it over the small children,*' he said firmly. '*They are weak and could die from this illness. I want them to have long, happy lives, like mine.*'

"His wisdom was great," she said, smiling fondly. She turned to Kenzi. "There is one other thing. Kenzi, in your story, the Mozzee family came here because they like our pond."

"Yes."

"Why is that?"

"I think it's because there are no fish," he replied. "If we had fish in the pond, they would eat up the mosquito larvae."

"How would you like to do a science experiment? Before Fizzee and her sisters start their own families, we could get some tilapia to live in the pond to eat the larvae in the water. Maybe the Mozzees will move away."

"Yes, tilapia! To catch and **eat**," said Moses, gleefully.

"I love fried tilapia," said Juma.

Kimana crossed her eyes and groaned.

"If we eat them all we won't have any to eat the larvae," she muttered. Lena and Abigail giggled.

"Quiet!" said Mrs Moyo. "And if the tilapia numbers grow into a big school of fish, then you *may* be able to catch and eat *some* of them."

At that moment there was a knock at the door. A small boy came in and gave Mrs Moyo a note.

"This is from the Principal," he said. As she read it, the bell rang.

"Before you go," said Mrs Moyo, "I have just received this message. It says: *Billy is nearly better and will be returning to school on Monday.*"

She looked at Kenzi. He was smiling joyfully from his left ear to his right.

"But now, let's clap our hands for Kenzi – and Ozzee."

The children clapped and cheered. Then they trooped outside to play. They put their arms out like wings, and charged about the playground yelling:

"EEEEAAAYOW!"

"BIYUZZZZZZZZ!"

"ZEEEYOOOOOM!"

— Just like little Mozzees.

The Ozzee Rap, Part Two

Getting caught in the net gave her such a big fright
That Ozzee refuses to hunt us and bite.
But her seven small sisters are all very good
At stealthy attack and sucking our blood.
So beware of MALARIA heading your way
If you don't keep those naughty MOZZEES at bay.

Key Words

ANOPHELES – The only kind of mosquito that **transmits** malaria. They bite us after sunset.

LARVA – Young form of mosquito with no wings, like a short worm, that lives in water. At about 10 days, **larvae** become mosquitoes.

MALARIA – *An illness caused by **parasites** that enter the body through the bite of an infected **anopheles mosquito**.*

MOSQUITO REPELLENT – Cream, oil or spray, to put on our skin, cloth or in the air, that frightens mosquitoes away or poisons them.

PARASITE – A smaller creature that lives in or on a bigger one, often making it weak or ill.

PROBOSCIS – A long tube extending from the mouth of the mosquito. It sucks up water or blood through the **proboscis.**

STANDING WATER – Water that does not flow or move, e.g. in ponds, puddles, water butts, old tyres. **Mosquitoes** lay their eggs here.

Author's Note

I was bitten by the idea of Ozzee and her Mozzee sisters while reading Wangari Maathai's book, *The Challenge for Africa,* in Kenya in 2022.

Malaria, she writes, is still one of the most serious challenges facing many African countries, and a particular danger to the very young. She writes of the need to educate people about methods of self-protection, especially the importance of small children sleeping under mosquito nets.

In the 1990s, living with my children in Addis Ababa, I had to keep us all safe when we travelled to malarial areas. Anti-malaria pills made us sick, but we were taught by others how to avoid getting bitten and we never caught it, though we often stayed out after dark, telling stories around the fire.

I hope this story will help to protect children and their families, in Africa and elsewhere, from the dangerous bites of Ozzee and her sisters.

I would like to thank: Hilary Platman for her good suggestions and hawk-eyed proofreading; Jock Bark for his inspired artwork and generosity with his time; and Oliver Tooley of Blue Poppy Publishing for his precision and sensitivity in preparation of this book and his patience with its author.

A Polite Request From the Publisher

As a very small publisher, we don't have a multi-million dollar marketing budget. So if you have enjoyed this book, or found it useful, we would be grateful if you could write a review or tell a friend.

Please feel free to be honest. We would sooner see plenty of sincere reviews with constructive criticism than a swathe of five-stars alongside empty platitudes like "… couldn't put it down".

If you know someone or some organisation that would find this book useful or enjoyable, please tell them.

Thank you.